Five Children's Stories
by Grandma

To James,
I hope you like
these stories ⌐

Love
Aunt Arlyne

Five Children's Stories by Grandma

Arlyne Parness

VANTAGE PRESS
New York

Illustrated by Tanya Stewart

FIRST EDITION

Published by Vantage Press, Inc.
419 Park Ave. South, New York, NY 10016

Manufactured in the United States of America
ISBN: 0-533-15269-0

Library of Congress Catalog Card No.: 2005905540

0 9 8 7 6 5 4 3 2 1

To our grandchildren,
Lizzie, Jonathan, Emerson, Andrew
and Brady
—The ultimate joys of our lives—

Contents

Five Children's Stories
by Grandma

When I Was Your Age . . .
I Was Just Your Size

When I was your age . . . there was no television.

So we listened to radio, read many books, and played lots of games.

When I was your age . . . there were no CDs or cassettes.

So we listened to records. They looked a bit like CDs but were bigger and they were black.

When I was your age . . . there were no colored markers.

So we drew pictures with crayons and colored pencils.

When I was your age . . . there were no microwave ovens.

So meals took hours to make. I talked to my mom while she cooked.

When I was your age . . . there was no Velcro.

So we learned how to tie our shoelaces.

When I was your age . . . there were no roller blades.

So we rode bikes, scooters, and roller skates.

When I was your age . . . there were no VCRs or DVD players.

But that was okay because there were no videos or DVDs.

When I was your age . . . there were no cell phones.

So we used pay phones, on the street, and had to put money into the phone each time we wanted to make a call.

When I was your age . . . there were no computers or E-mail.

So we wrote letters by hand, put them into stamped envelopes and placed them into the mailbox on the street. The mailman delivered them. You call that "snail mail."

When I was your age . . . there was no Internet.

So we went to the library to look up information in books.

When I was your age . . . there were no malls.

So we shopped in small neighborhood stores.

But we did have lots of books.

We learned to use our imaginations, figured things out, and invented all the great stuff you have now.

Then one day we had television.

But we still didn't have clickers.

"No, Dear, Not with a Stranger!"

"Mommy, is it ever safe to go into a car, alone, with a stranger?"

"No, dear, it is not. Not for any reason."

"Even if he says, your mommy or your daddy or your nanny or your grandma or your grandpa or anyone else told me to pick you up?"

"No, dear, not with a stranger."

"Even if he says, I have a new puppy or a little kitten in my car. Do you want to see it?"

"No, dear, not with a stranger."

"Even if he says, please help, help me, I need your help?"

"No, dear, not with a stranger."

"Even if he says, I have some treats for you. I have ice cream, candy, cookies, want some?"

"No, dear, not with a stranger."

"Even if he says, I have a surprise for you in my car. Come here so I can give it to you?"

"No, dear, not with a stranger."

"Even if he says, I am a safe person. It is okay for you to come to my car. Your mommy said it is okay?"

"No, dear, not with a stranger."

"Even if he says, I know your family password, but I just can't think of it right now?"

"No, dear, not with a stranger."

"Even if he says, you remember me, I work with your mommy or your daddy or anyone else I know?"

"No, dear, not with a stranger."

"Is it ever safe to go into a car with a stranger?"

"NO, NOT EVER."

Uh Oh, My Tooth Is Loose

Lizzie woke up and went straight to the bathroom. She really had to hurry this morning or she would be late for school. This wasn't just any school day, this was Lizzie's *first* day in *first grade.*

Lizzie washed her hands and face, then took her toothbrush in her hand and began to apply the toothpaste. She touched her teeth with her tongue.

Uh oh, that feels funny, thought Lizzie. She began to brush and noticed that one of her bottom teeth was moving. Lizzie felt her tooth with her finger and realized this was her *first loose tooth.*

Hmmm, the *first* day of *first* grade and her *first* loose tooth. Wow, what a day! Lizzie rushed to show her mother, who agreed this was, indeed, a special day. Lizzie was so excited but she knew she had to continue to get ready for school, quickly.

All day long Lizzie played with her loose tooth by wiggling it with her tongue. It didn't really wiggle much but Lizzie knew it was moving. It was a fun day.

Lizzie liked her new teacher and she liked the kids in her new class. There were four kids in her class who had already lost some teeth. Lizzie was sure she would be next.

At the end of her first day, Lizzie got on the school bus with a smile on her face. She had a secret. Lizzie was sure that she would be the next one in her class to lose a tooth.

Each morning, Lizzie got up and checked her tooth. She wiggled it with her tongue and then with her finger. After five days passed, she was puzzled. *When is this tooth going to come out?* she asked herself.

Another five days passed and then another five days. *Will this tooth ever come out?* she wondered.

Weeks passed by, then a month. Still her tooth had not fallen out. Lizzie's mother said, "This will teach you patience, sweetheart, and that's a very important thing to learn."

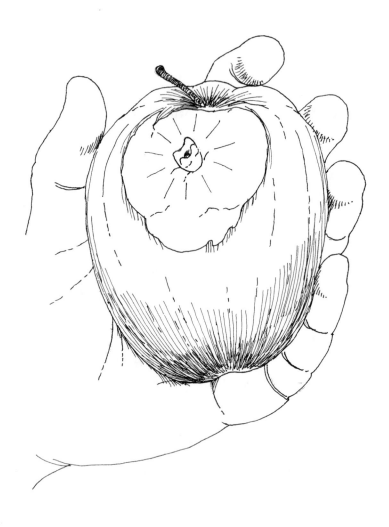

The next day, during snack time in school, Lizzie was eating an apple. All of a sudden, it happened. It really happened! Her tooth was in the apple . . . really, in the apple! It finally happened!

Lizzie ran to the mirror. *Cool,* she thought. It felt so funny but she felt so good. *This is the best day ever,* thought Lizzie. Now she knew she was really growing up.

Lizzie showed her first empty tooth space to all her friends and they were very happy for her. Carefully, she wrapped her tooth in a tissue and put it into her backpack, to take it home to show her mother.

Lizzie's mother was excited and took a picture of Lizzie with her first missing tooth.

"Make sure you put your tooth under your pillow, sweetheart, so that the tooth fairy can find it," said Mother. Lizzie did just that.

The next morning, Lizzie woke up early. It wasn't even light out yet. But that didn't matter to Lizzie. She quickly reached under her pillow to see what the tooth fairy had left her. It was the perfect gift, a beautiful new diary and a matching pen.

This is so cool, thought Lizzie. Then, out loud, she said, "This is the year that I learn to write sentences. I will write about how it feels to lose your first tooth. Maybe it will even become a book."

Bigger Isn't Better, It's Just Bigger!

It was Emerson's first day of school. She was a bit scared. Would she like her teacher? Would she like the children in her class? Would they like her?

Emerson was very kind and she was very smart. She even knew all the letters in the alphabet and lots of numbers.

She could sing and she knew how to hang up her own jacket.

But, could she leave her mom?

When she got to school, the first person she met was her teacher, Carrie. Carrie was very cool. She introduced Emerson to the other children in the class.

"How old are you, Emerson?" asked Brian.

"I am four years old. How old are you?" she replied.

"I am four years old, too, but I am bigger than you," Brian said, "so I am better than you."

Emerson began to cry. She ran to her mother and told her what Brian had said.

"Mommy, is Brian really better than I am?"

"No, sweetheart," said her mother. "Bigger isn't better, it's just BIGGER!"

Carrie took Emerson's hand and brought her to meet the other kids. She met Andrew, Brady, Harry, and Emma. Andrew was playing with trucks and trains. Brady was playing music on the piano. Emma was reading her book and Harry was on the trampoline.

"What would you like to play with, Emerson?" asked Carrie.

"I want to play with paints," said Emerson.

Carrie showed Emerson where the paints were and gave her lots of paper, brushes, wipes, and a place to call her own. Emerson began to mix some colors and paint great pictures on her paper.

Brian saw what Emerson was doing and asked if he could watch.

Emerson said, "OK, Brian, but please don't mess up my painting."

"I won't, I promise," he replied.

She began to tell Brian about the painting. Emerson said she was making a picture of all the kids in their class.

Brian looked at the painting and asked, "Where am I?"

"Oh, you're not in the picture."

"Why not?" he asked.

"You're too big, and there isn't enough room," replied Emerson.

Thinking Moments
("If You Can't Change a Situation, Change Your Attitude Towards It")

"Grandma's coming, Grandma's coming," shouted Jonathan. "I love when Grandma comes to our house."

"I know you do," said Mother. "You get so excited when you know she's coming. What is your favorite part of Grandma's visits?" she asked.

"Actually, I love the *thinking moments* best," he replied.

"What do you mean by *thinking moments?*" Mother asked.

"You know, Mom, that's the time when Grandma and I sit in our special chair, all alone, and she asks her special questions."

"What kind of special questions does she ask you?"

"Grandma asks me things that make me think a lot," he replied.

"Can you give me an example of a *Thinking Moment* question?" asked Mother.

"Um, yes, she asks me questions like . . . What is something I like a lot about myself?"

"How did you answer that question, Jonathan?" Mother asked.

"I really had to think about that one, but Grandma told me I don't have to answer the *thinking moment* questions right away . . . that's why they are called *thinking moment* questions . . . so I can think about them. But, I think I know the answer . . . one of the things I like about me is that I really love to learn new things."

"I like that a lot about you, too, Jonathan," said his mother.

"Mommy, Grandma asks me lots of *thinking moment* questions, like . . . what don't I like about myself and is it something I can change? Or . . . what do I like most about my best friend and why is that important to me?"

Mother asked, "What is the best thing you have learned from Grandma?"

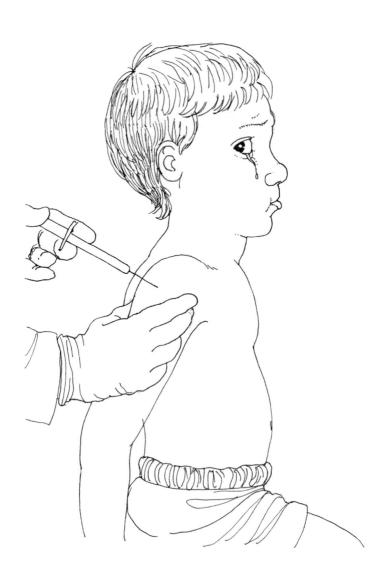

Jonathan replied, "One time Grandma asked me what I did not like about going to the doctor. I told her that I didn't like getting shots. Grandma asked if I could change the situation? I said, 'No, because the doctor said it is a necessary part of my check-up.'

"Then Grandma had a *thinking moment* and she asked, 'Do you know why it is necessary?' "

" 'Yes,' I said, 'because it keeps me from getting sick.' "

" 'Well then,' said Grandma, 'Maybe you need to change your attitude towards it and then it will not bother you.' "

"I asked Grandma what that meant and she said, 'It means that you should try to find the good things about the situation, and if you do, then the situation will become something you like instead of something you don't like.' I sort of got mixed up at first, but Grandma explained it more. 'It's like, if your team loses a soccer game, you're sad . . . but if you didn't play because you thought you might lose, then you wouldn't have the fun of playing at all.' "

"I see," said Mother. "So, what you're saying is . . . if we find the good parts of things and think about *them* instead of the bad parts, we will really be happier people. You know what I think, Jonathan? I think Grandma is pretty smart."

"Yup, so do I."